THE SLY SPY

By Marjorie and Mitchell Sharmat:

Olivia Sharp, Agent for Secrets:
THE PIZZA MONSTER
THE PRINCESS OF THE FILLMORE STREET SCHOOL

By Marjorie Weinman Sharmat:

Nate the Great:
NATE THE GREAT
NATE THE GREAT AND THE BORING BEACH BAG
NATE THE GREAT AND THE LOST LIST
NATE THE GREAT AND THE MISSING KEY
NATE THE GREAT AND THE PHONY CLUE
NATE THE GREAT AND THE SNOWY TRAIL
NATE THE GREAT STALKS STUPIDWEED
NATE THE GREAT AND THE STICKY CASE
NATE THE GREAT GOES UNDERCOVER
NATE THE GREAT AND THE FISHY PRIZE

THE SON OF THE SLIME WHO ATE CLEVELAND

By Mitchell Sharmat:

COME HOME, WILMA
GREGORY, THE TERRIBLE EATER
A GIRL OF MANY PARTS
REDDY RATTLER AND EASY EAGLE
SHERMAN IS A SLOWPOKE
THE SEVEN SLOPPY DAYS OF PHINEAS PIG

THE SLY SPY

by Marjorie and Mitchell Sharmat

Illustrated by
Denise Brunkus

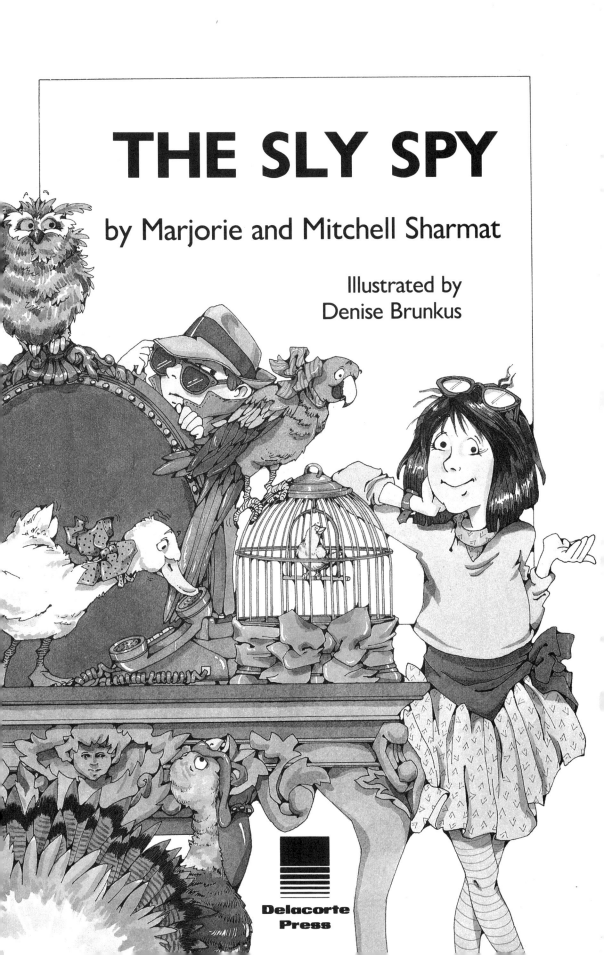

Delacorte
Press

For Craig
—— M.S. and M.S.

For Sally Lang
—— D.B.

Published by
Delacorte Press
Bantam Doubleday Dell Publishing Group, Inc.
666 Fifth Avenue
New York, New York 10103

Library of Congress Cataloging in Publication Data

Sharmat, Marjorie Weinman.
   The sly spy / by Marjorie Sharmat and Mitchell
Sharmat; illustrated by Denise Brunkus.
      p.   cm.—(Olivia Sharp, agent for secrets)
   Summary: E.J. the spy tries to uncover a secret that
Olivia is keeping for a client.
   ISBN 0-385-29974-5
   [1. Secrets—Fiction. 2. Spies—Fiction.] I. Sharmat,
Mitchell. II. Brunkus, Denise, ill. III. Title. IV. Series:
Sharmat, Marjorie Weinman. Olivia Sharp, agent for
secrets.
PZ7.S5299S1 1990
[E]—dc20   89-23335
                                                    CIP
                                                     AC
Manufactured in the United States of America

April 1990

10 9 8 7 6 5 4 3 2 1

LBM

My name is Olivia Sharp.
I'm an agent for secrets.
If you have a secret problem, call me.
I work out of my penthouse on top of
Pacific Heights in San Francisco.

Let me tell you about my last case. It began on a Saturday.

The week had been slow. The red phone in my office hadn't rung in days. My desk was clean. I was trying to figure out what I could do to drum up business.

I decided to hit the streets and see who I could find who needed help.

I grabbed my boa and rang for my chauffeur, Willie, to bring the limo around.

Then I went to the elevator and pressed the button.

When the elevator came I stepped inside.

There was a boy standing in the corner.

The elevator started down. The boy slid his eyes sideways to look me over.

I had never seen him before. I could hardly see him now. A big hat was pulled down over his face. He was wearing a raincoat, even though it wasn't raining. He looked like *he* needed help. With his clothes, if nothing else.

"My name is Olivia Sharp," I said.

"Hello, Liver."

We were *not* off to a good start!

"I'm an agent for secrets," I said. "You may have heard of me. I'm almost famous. Here's my card."

"That's stupid," he said. He pushed his hat up. He had green eyes that glittered like a Halloween cat's.

"*Stupid* is a stupid word," I said. I fluffed my boa and turned my back on him.

When the elevator reached the ground floor, he just stood there. Maybe he lived in the elevator. I didn't want to. I got out.

Willie was waiting at the curb with the limo.

"Where to, Boss?" he asked as we rolled out of the courtyard, through the big iron gates, and onto Steiner Street.

"Cruise the streets. We're looking for clients, Willie."

Twenty minutes later I spotted some kids going into the grocery store on Union Street. "Pull over," I said.

I went into the grocery store while Willie parked the limo. I headed for the vegetable department. You can get a good view of the store from there.

I was turning over some mushrooms when someone tapped me on the shoulder.

I knew it was Sheena, even before I looked. All I had to do was sniff. Sheena uses a shampoo that smells like macaroons.

"Am I glad you're here!" she said. "I need your help."

I didn't want to let on that I was desperate for a new case. And besides, it doesn't look classy to pick up clients while you're feeling vegetables.

"**W**hat kind of help?" I asked coolly.

Sheena leaned closer to me. "It's about Desiree's birthday. Duncan, Mortimer, and I told Desiree we wanted to chip in for one nice present for her party tomorrow. We asked her for a hint about what she'd like. She said, 'I love feathers.' So we bought Desiree a canary."

"A *canary*?"

"Yes. A canary has lots of feathers."

"Right. So what's the secret problem?"

"The canary is. We want the canary to be a secret until Desiree's party. Mortimer took it home. But Desiree went to his house and started looking around. That's not fair! A secret is supposed to be a secret."

"I guess Desiree just can't wait to see what you got her. But if she finds out she'll spoil her own surprise. She didn't see the canary, did she?"

Sheena smiled. "No, it was lucky that Duncan had come by to take it out for a walk."

"*D*uncan took a canary for a *walk*?" I couldn't believe what I was hearing. I lifted my boa out of a bin of broccoli.

"Yes. Duncan says canaries need fresh air. So he took it out, cage and all."

"Go on."

"Well, since Desiree had been snooping around Mortimer's house, Duncan said he'd keep the canary at *his* house."

"That didn't solve your problem?" I asked.

"No. Desiree went to Duncan's house! Good thing I was there. I grabbed the canary cage and sneaked down the back stairs before Desiree could see the canary and me. And here we are!"

"*We?*"

Sheena pointed to the floor. Behind her was a canary in a cage! Sheena kept pointing. "I can't take him home because I know Desiree will come over. She'll keep going to Mortimer's and Duncan's and my house until she catches one of us with the canary."

"Let me get this straight," I said. "Your problem is that you have no place to keep the canary until Desiree's birthday party?"

"That's it," Sheena said. "This can be your new case."

This was a *case*? No way.

It was a thousand yawns!

 B ut I wanted to help Sheena and Mortimer and Duncan.

"I'm good with birds," I said. "I already have my pet owl, Hoot. And I have lots of room. I'll keep the canary until Desiree's party tomorrow. And I'll keep it a secret."

Sheena handed me the birdcage. "His name is Feathers. He's named for Desiree's hint."

"Good to know," I said.

Sheena started to walk away.

I said, "I usually don't do business over vegetables. I have an office, I have a desk, I have files, I have a red telephone. I have ads all over town with my telephone number on them."

I pointed to the bulletin board near the front of the store. "I even have an ad in this store."

"Not anymore," Sheena said. "I checked for it, but it's gone."

"Gone? How can it be gone?"

Sheena shrugged and walked away.

I rushed to the bulletin board. I looked at the spot where I had put up my ad. I saw an ad. But it wasn't mine! It said:

I lifted a corner of the ad and looked under it.

My ad was still there! Hidden. This E.J. person had covered it up.

I pulled down E.J.'s ad and put it in my pocketbook. *I* was going to call 555-4133! There was plenty of room for both of our ads, so why had E.J. covered *mine?*

I left the store with the canary and the spy ad.

"Nice bird, Boss," Willie said.

Willie drove us home.

The elevator was empty this time. Maybe Mr. Stupid had a hobby of riding in elevators and he had gone on to another building. I could only hope.

I introduced Feathers to my house-keeper, Mrs. Fridgeflake.

"We have an overnight guest," I said.

Then I went to Hoot's room and said, "I've got a friend for you, Hoot."

Hoot looked at Feathers. It was not a friendly look.

I decided to give Feathers his own room.

I put him in the yellow room, which matched his feathers. It's my parents' room, but I knew they wouldn't mind since they were in Stockholm, Sweden, that week. I wished they would come home soon.

"This room belongs to Wilfred and Maude. They're my parents," I said to Feathers. "So behave yourself."

I went to my office to call 555-4133.

But my red telephone rang first.

Maybe a real client at last!

"Olivia Sharp, Agent for Secrets," I answered. "Your world is coming to an end," a voice said. It was Duncan.

"*My* world is coming to an end?" I asked.

"Yes. I just saw four of your ads covered over with some kind of spy ad. Now you're the one who has a problem. Can I help?"

"*Four* of my ads?"

This was spreading! Pretty soon all my ads would be hidden. Maybe they were already.

No wonder business was bad!

"I'll look into it," I said. "Thanks."

I put down the receiver. Then I picked it up and dialed 555-4133.

After the fifth ring I heard a boy's voice announce, "This is E.J.'s Spy Service. I will be glad to spy for you, but I am not here right now. Leave your number."

An answering machine! I refuse to talk to machines. I slammed down the receiver.

I went to my furry white chair, sat down, and looked out the window. There was no fog over San Francisco Bay, and I could see the boats moving back and forth past Alcatraz Island.

I thought about the boy's voice on the answering machine. The sound of the *s* in *Spy* and *Service.* I had heard that *s* before. But where?

I sank deeper into my chair. But not for long. I heard *chirp, chirp, chirp.*

Feathers was chirping away.

Chirp, chirp, chirp. Nonstop. Noisy bird!

That's what I like about an owl. They only give a hoot now and then.

Maybe Feathers was hungry. What do you feed a canary?

I grabbed my boa and the canary cage. I rang for Willie to bring the limo around.

"To the Feathered Friends Pet Shop," I said as I settled into the backseat with Feathers.

It only took five minutes to get there. Feathers chirped all the way.

The store was full of feathery pets.

One of them looked like my boa.

I made my way past a goose, a duck, a chicken, a parrot, and a canary.

I held up my canary cage.

"I'll have one day's supply of whatever this creature eats," I said to a lady behind a counter.

I bought the pet food and fed Feathers on the spot.

Then we went home.

Willie parked the limo while I got into the elevator with Feathers.

M r. Stupid was there!

He pulled his collar up and his hat down.

"Is that your canary?" he asked as the elevator started up.

"This isn't a canary," I said. "This is actually an elephant, pretending to be a canary."

"That's stupid," he said.

"Just a minute," I said. "That's two stupids too many. Who do you think you are, anyway?"

The elevator jerked to a stop at the fourth floor.

"So long, Liver," he said, and he got off.

He walked to the door of the apartment just opposite the elevator. My best friend, Taffy Plimpton, had lived in that apartment before she moved away to Carmel. Mr. Stupid must have moved in!

"Wait!" I called.

But the elevator door closed.

Suddenly I knew who he *really* was! When he said *stupid,* the *s* had leapt up and nudged my brain. *S* as in Spy Service. This boy was E.J., the person who had covered my ads and spoiled my business!

When the elevator reached my floor, I went straight to my office and dialed 555-4133.

This time E.J. answered. "E.J. the spy, who's sly, at your service."

"This is Olivia Sharp, Agent for Secrets, and I know yours. You live on the fourth floor of my building."

"So what," he said.

"So this," I said. "You've been going around town covering up my ads. Why?"

"You're an agent for secrets. I'm a spy. You figure it out."

I figured it out and I didn't like it.

"Can't talk," he said. "I'm busy with a big case."

This kid was unreal. I yawned and said, "Oh, really? You've got an actual case?"

"Right. So long, Liver."

He hung up.

I don't believe in war, but E.J. was beginning to give the idea a good name. He hadn't heard the last from me.

I went to my room to paint my toenails.

I was on nail number four when the doorbell rang.

I padded out to the door and opened it.

Mortimer was standing there, looking scared. That's his regular look. I wish I could help him with that, but he hasn't asked me.

"It's my turn to take Feathers for his walk," he said. "We're going to Alta Plaza Park."

I got Feathers and handed the cage to Mortimer. "You two enjoy your walk."

I went back to my toenails.

I was giving nail number two a second coat when the doorbell rang.

Mortimer was back. He tiptoed in and closed the door.

"A kid with a big hat followed me down in the elevator," he said. "He asked me who the canary belonged to. I didn't tell him."

I laughed. "That's E.J. He thinks he's a spy. He's new in the building."

"He's new at school too," Mortimer said. "I've seen him talking to Desiree a lot."

"Oh, no!" I said. "We're in big trouble. I bet Desiree *hired* him to find out what her feathered present from you and Sheena and Duncan is. And now he's seen you with Feathers!"

"And he's waiting to see me some more," Mortimer said. "He's downstairs, hiding behind a planter."

Now I knew I had a *real* case! And I knew what I had to do.

I grabbed Feathers's cage. "Feathers is staying in," I said. "You're taking *Hoot* to the park. Lead the spy *away* from this building. If he asks you about Hoot, tell him you've got a bird-walking service."

I got Hoot, gave her to Mortimer, and pushed him out the door.

There wasn't time to start a file on the case. I rang for Willie.

"Back to the Feathered Friends Pet Shop," I said as I stepped into the limo.

When we got to the pet store I dashed inside, pointing in all directions.

"Do you rent?" I asked. "Never mind, I'll take one of each."

I got back in the limo with a duck, a parrot, and a turkey.

"You're going overboard for birds, Boss," Willie said as the duck tried to waddle around the front seat.

Back home I had Willie check to make sure the elevator was empty.

E.J. was not in sight.

The birds and I made the trip to the top without any problems, except for some squawking and quacking.

Mrs. Fridgeflake eyed them nervously. "More overnight guests?"

I put the birds in the blue room in back. "I'll come for you soon," I promised them, and I closed the door.

Ten minutes later Mortimer rang the bell. "We were followed every step of the way," he whispered. "Is our secret safe or unsafe?"

"Soon it will be safe," I said.

Mortimer handed Hoot to me and left.

I put Hoot in the yellow room with Feathers. "No fighting," I warned.

I went to my office, grabbed my red telephone, and dialed 555-4133.

"E.J.'s Spy Service," a voice answered. "This is E.J."

"This is Olivia Sharp."

"Hi, Liver. I know one of your secrets."

"Do you?"

"Sure. That's my job. Mortimer, Sheena, and Duncan got a birthday present for Desiree and you're keeping it for them."

I tapped a pencil on my desk. "Am I?"

"Listen, Liver. Desiree hinted for a present with feathers. And they got her a canary. Or an owl. Either way it's a pretty weird birthday present, if you ask me."

"I didn't ask. And don't you dare come up here to look around!"

I slammed down the receiver.

I was smiling. I knew it wouldn't be long before my doorbell rang.

It wasn't.

He was there at the door, big hat and all.

"Stay out," I said, leaving the door open wide enough for him to squeeze his way in. He was now dealing, face-to-face, with Olivia Sharp, Agent for Secrets.

E.J. started to walk around my penthouse.

Chirping sounds and hoots were coming from the yellow room.

He headed straight for it, walked in, and saw Feathers and Hoot. "*One* of these is Desiree's present," he said. "All I have to do is figure out which one."

I slipped away while E.J. went on talking.

I walked down the hall, opened the door to the blue room, and said, "Okay, birds, you're free!" I was back before E.J. knew I was gone. He was still staring at Hoot, then Feathers, then back at Hoot again. A duck waddled past me into the room, quacking happily. Behind it a turkey gobble-gobbled. A parrot flew in, squawking. Feathers chirped. Hoot kept her beak shut. Sometimes she's so stuck up.

E.J. looked from the duck to the turkey to the parrot and then back to the canary and owl.

I *love* confusion, especially when I cause it.

E.J. did not know which bird was the present!

My plan had worked, the secret was safe.

E.J. pushed his hat back. "Clever work, Liver, but I still know the present is a *bird*. So there!"

I had to think fast.

I said, "Let's go to my office."

I think faster there.

I led the way.

"Nice place," E.J. said, fingering my red phone.

We sat down.

E.J. was chuckling. "A bird is a really weird present," he said. "Especially if it's a turkey. Weird presents are the greatest. I wanted to get Desiree something weird but I couldn't find anything."

I looked E.J. straight in the eye. "What *are* you giving Desiree for her birthday?"

He squirmed. Then he said, "That's my secret until she opens it. I want her to be surprised."

"See?" I said. "Even *you* know that birthday secrets should be kept."

I leaned toward him. "Listen to me, E.J. I don't know how long you've been a spy, but there are some cases you shouldn't take. You think *I* take every case that comes along?"

So far I had. But they were all good causes.

I put my feet up on my desk. "We both want Desiree to have a happy birthday, right?"

E.J. was staring or glaring at me. Hard to tell which.

"I worked hard on this case," he said. "You want me to drop it?"

"Your choice." I pointed to my red phone. "You can use this to call Desiree."

I tapped my fingers on my desk while E.J. dialed. Was he going to spill the bird secret?

It seemed to take forever for Desiree to answer.

Then E.J. spoke into the phone. "E.J's Spy Service reporting in," he said. "I finished the case. Got the big answer. You'll love this, Desiree. Your birthday present is—"

I didn't want to hear it!

"WEIRD!" he announced. "Glad I could be of help."

E.J. hung up.

He wasn't so bad after all.

I invited him for tea. He took off his hat and stayed.

He called me Liver twice, but I let it pass.

After he left, I went to my office and called Sheena.

"All's well," I said.

For her and Duncan and Mortimer it was. For me, I had to plan a future for a duck, a turkey, and a parrot.

I started and finished a file on the case.
This is how I ended it:

* TOMORROW DESIREE IS GETTING
  A CANARY FROM SHEENA,
  DUNCAN AND MORTIMER.

* SHE'S GETTING BANGLES
  FROM ME AND A PIN WITH
  HER NAME ON IT FROM E·J.
** HE DOESN'T KNOW I SAW
  THE ORDER FORM
  STICKING OUT OF HIS POCKET.

E·J. HAS A LOT MORE TO
  LEARN ABOUT BEING A SPY.
  AND A FRIEND.

MAYBE I'LL TEACH HIM.

MAYBE I WON'T.

About the Authors

MITCHELL SHARMAT and MARJORIE WEINMAN SHARMAT have written several children's books together and numerous books individually. The award-winning authors have now teamed up to create an original and amazing new series about Olivia Sharp, a helpful, problem-solving grade-school heroine who is in business for herself as an agent for secrets.

Marjorie Sharmat was born and grew up in Portland, Maine. She has been writing since age eight and is the author of nearly a hundred books. She is probably best known as the creator of the world-famous sleuth Nate the Great. Mitchell Sharmat, a native of Brookline, Massachusetts, and a graduate of Harvard, is active in real estate and stock market investments when he's not writing books. His wildly popular *Gregory, the Terrible Eater,* a Reading Rainbow featured selection, has become a children's classic.

The Sharmats live in Tucson, Arizona. They have two grown sons, Craig and Andrew.

About the Illustrator

DENISE BRUNKUS has illustrated several books for children. She lives in Hunterdon County, New Jersey, with her husband, young daughter, and otterhound.